The
Freaky Joe
Club

Illustrated by
John Manders

The Freaky Joe Club

Secret File #2:

The Case of the Smiling Shark

by
P. J. McMahon

ALADDIN PAPERBACKS
New York   London   Toronto   Sydney

To the one, the true, the only Bella —P. J. M.

This book is a work of fiction. Any references to historical events, real people, or real locales are used fictitiously. Other names, characters, places, and incidents are the product of the author's imagination, and any resemblance to actual events or locales or persons, living or dead, is entirely coincidental.

First Aladdin Paperbacks edition May 2004

Text copyright © 2004 by Patricia McMahon
Illustrations copyright © 2004 by John Manders

ALADDIN PAPERBACKS
An imprint of Simon & Schuster Children's Publishing Division
1230 Avenue of the Americas, New York, NY 10020

Designed by Lisa Vega
The text of this book was set in 14-point Minion.
Printed in the United States of America
10 9 8 7 6 5 4 3 2 1

Library of Congress Control Number 2004102699
ISBN 0-689-86261-X

Table of Contents

The Case of the
Smiling Shark

Chapter One

A Terrible Tale, or Two

The time has come. I, Conor, code name The Condor, will record the tale of our second adventure. This is the task given to me as the founder of this club, and the one who was told of Freaky Joe.

Yes, I am the one who must show my companions the true road a crime fighter must follow.

Oh, and that true crime fighters should try not to damage each other.

Or animals.

Or small children.

Basically anyone.

And by the way, club members should be loyal to one another. Should remember that we are the good guys. So we don't get one another in trouble.

My task is not an easy one.

I pick up the book. Large, red, chewed in one corner and bound with a bicycle chain, it has bold, black letters across the cover.

THE SECRET FILES OF THE
FREAKY JOE CLUB:
DO NOT OPEN UNLESS YOU ARE
A MEMBER OR ELSE.

I chew the end of my pencil. Riley, The Beast, chews the end of my shoelace. Where to begin, where to begin. Can I truly tell the tale of those hot summer days? (It is always really hot here in Texas in the summer.)

When in doubt, follow Freaky Joe's advice: Rule Number Three B: Begin at the Beginning. Which would be in The Secret Place one morning.

. . . .

I sit happily on the soccer ball beanbag chair, my feet up on the baseball beanbag chair. Except for Riley, I am alone this morning. Swim team practice begins soon, and I'll have to go. But now, balancing a book on my knees, I read. The excitement is almost killing me.

Remington Reedmarsh, Lemur Detective, the hero of my favorite series, is in an awful spot. He has taken refuge in a ruined castle. The forces of The Terrible Tyrant Tyler, a Marsupial of Enormous Size, are massing to attack the castle. Everyone is silent, waiting, till—*BANG!*

The door to The Secret Place crashes open.

The door handle knocks a hole in the exact spot of the hole I just fixed.

3

"Jack! What are you doing?" I ask. My voice could be friendlier.

Jack stands in the door, a large towel wrapped around his head like a turban.

"I'm getting here before Timmy," he explains. "We called each other, counted to three." Jack snaps his fingers three times. "Hung up, and raced here."

He spreads his arms wide. "Ta da!"

"Ta da?" I ask. "Does 'Ta da' mean 'I broke the door'?"

"Uh. No." Jack looks at the new hole. Where he himself had made the first hole. "Oops."

Oops? Somehow breaking the wall, again, deserves more than an oops. Before I can think of something to say, the door flies open again.

Timmy races in so fast he knocks Jack to the ground and lands on top of him. He is wearing a towel around his body like some strange strapless dress.

I close *Remington Reedmarsh and the Terrible Tyrant.* This is the end of my reading.

"You won!" Timmy says in disgust.

"I won," Jack agrees. At least I think that is what he said. He might have said "Saigon" or "Ho hum." Difficult to be sure what he means when he is buried under Timmy.

Riley is not sure what he is saying. Or what he is doing under Timmy. She licks his face to let him know.

"Ooooooh, yuck!" Jack yells. Quite clearly.

"Hello, Riley girl." Timmy pulls what looks like a pretzel out of his back pocket and gives half to Riley.

"Don't feed her too much," I tell Timmy. "My mom says she is getting too plump."

"Plump?" Jack asks, making the last *p* pop.

"If she's too plump, it's not our fault," Timmy says.

We all turn. A newspaper picture, blown up

and mounted, hangs on the wall next to a goril-la mask.

Bubba Butowski, ace security guard of our neighborhood, Ship's Cove, smiles out at the camera happily. By his side, Riley sits smiling with a large dog bone in her mouth.

LOCAL SECURITY GUARD BREAKS UP BICYCLE THEFT RING

"I could not have done it without this great dog," the text reads. He could not have done it without us. In fact he did not do it. We did. The members of the Freaky Joe Club. (See *Secret File #1: The Mystery of the Swimming Gorilla*.)

"Bubba is the one who makes Riley plump. Bubba gives Riley treats. Which makes Riley too plump." Jack pops all his *p*'s. "Bubba gives Riley treats because Bubba loves . . ."

"Jack, stop," I suggest. But I'm too late.

Riley knows that name. She tilts her head. I can

see her doggie brain thinking, *Bubba? Where?* She runs. Barks. Runs. Barks. Stopping now and then to lick Jack's face. And then barks again.

"Now look what you've done, Jack." Timmy corrals Riley, giving her half of his previously chewed pretzel.

"Timmy, that is gross," Jack moans. He rolls from side to side.

Somehow, all this is not as exciting as facing down a Marsupial of Enormous Size.

"Riley doesn't think so," Timmy notices.

"Get off me, anyway," Jack says, squirming. "I want to be first at swim team practice today."

He worms out from under Timmy. "Let's go. Pablo is going to give Sam a hand. And I think I'll be ready to do it tomorrow."

"No way," Timmy says.

"Yes way." Jack does a little dance. "Oh, way. Big way."

And then he flies out the door. Shouting "Octopi! Octopi!" His turban unravels as he goes.

"Come on, Conor!" Timmy yells. My house backs up to the pool, so my mom put a gate in the back. All our friends use it.

"Be a good Beast," I tell Riley. "And guard The Secret Place." Riley tilts her head to the side. Listening.

I follow along. As I come through the gate, an unknown adult waves and waves at me. And heads into the pool.

I wonder who that was. I also wonder, will I ever get to give Sam a hand? I'm not sure even Freaky Joe has the answer to that question.

Chapter Two

Give the Man a Hand

Wheeewww!

A whistle blows as I push open the high metal gate into the Ship's Cove pool.

And blows again.

Coach Greta loves her whistle. And she uses it. A lot. I think as a little girl she wanted to grow up to blow a whistle. So she became head coach of the Octopi, the Ship's Cove swim team. Which is her summer job. In the winter, she drives a cement truck.

"Okay, every-one calm down," Coach Greta insists.

"And someone clean those pinecones out of the bottom of the pool."

Ten swimmers dive in to clean up three pinecones.

"Hey, Condor," Jack yells from the end of the pool. He and Timmy carry a full-size cardboard person.

"It's *The* Condor," Timmy tells him in a very loud voice. "And it's supposed to be a secret."

Luckily few people hear him as a very loud whistle blows again. Three times for luck.

Freaky Joe is right. Rule Number Seventeen C: Sometimes Code Names Are Too Much Trouble. Go to Rule Number Seventeen D.

Time to have an official Freaky Joe Club meeting.

"Set 'im up boys," Coach Greta calls.

Timmy and Jack stand up a life-size picture of General Sam Houston, hero of the Texas Revolution. At least if you were rooting for the

Texas side. He was also the first president of the Republic of Texas. The man who gave his name to our city. I'm not sure what his talents were as a swimmer.

He stands waiting at the end of the pool. He leans slightly, one hand down toward the water. The other hand holds a sign saying **SAM LOVES OCTOPI. SAM HATES SHARKS.**

"Ready to go, Pablo?" Greta asks.

Assistant Coach Pablo, a very tall, very skinny high school student, runs in place. He lifts his knees higher and higher, faster and faster. My sister, Bella, and her best friend, Mugsy, run alongside him. Pablo hops from one foot to the other. Ditto Bella and Mugsy.

The unknown adult type person I saw from outside the pool stands ready with a clipboard.

"Okey dokey, let 'er rip," Greta orders as Pablo dives into the pool. He swims to Sam, slaps the extended hand. And swims back. And back again.

The Octopi cheer. "Go, Pablo. Go, Pablo." Good strong cheers. By the tenth lap, the octopi cheer "Go, Go." Or "Pablo, Pablo." Soon they are down to one "Go." One "Pablo."

Then Mad Dog, whose mother named him Charley, yells "How Much Water!" The crowd takes up the cheer. For a lap or two.

Pablo will swim one hundred laps. I don't think we have one hundred laps of cheers in us.

This summer the ORCA Swim League (Our

Radiant Children are Athletes) has decided to help raise money for the new Sam Houston Memorial Pool and State History Center.

Each swimmer on each swim team asks people to pay him or her to swim laps of the pool. Back and forth, back and forth. Each team was given a Sam Houston. He is supposed to inspire the swimmers. I think ours is the only one that has the sign about the Octopi.

The money raised goes to Sam's Pool and School, as my mother calls it. And the team that raises the most money gets a trip to How Much Water?, a water park with pools, rides, and, well, a lot of water. Which everyone agrees would be pretty good.

And the coach of the winning team gets to go

to the grand opening of the Sam Houston Memorial Pool and State History Center. Which Coach Greta seems to think would be pretty good.

The day Sam came to the pool, Coach Greta was all fired up.

"Let's beat those Sharks! They always win these contests. Let's show everyone what the Octopi are made of! Whattaya say, kids? Can we do it? Can we do it?"

Coach Greta had us chanting "We can do it. We can do it."

"All right, here's the deal." Greta explained her plan of attack. "No one shakes Sam's hand unless they have ten sponsors. No getting in the pool with five dollars promised from your Uncle Bob. Each of you gets ten sponsors, and we raise more money than anyone else! Come on, kids! I know we can beat those Sharks. I promise you." Coach Greta crossed her heart.

"Beat the Sharks! Beat the Sharks!"

It was wild. I thought a volcano was going to erupt any minute.

And before we knew it, we all agreed to find ten sponsors before we would Give Sam a Hand.

Right now, I have one. My mom. And she is not going to break the bank for Sam's Pool and School, as she calls it. And going door to door, grubbing money from the neighbors, is not something my mother wants me to do. Whatever grubbing is.

I don't know how I am going to find ten sponsors. And if I don't, will that keep the team from winning? From going to How Much Water? And then the Sharks will win. The Sharks! All because of me.

My thoughts of doom are interrupted by that lovely whistle sound.

"Okey dokey, that's enough watching," Coach Great orders. "Let's see some swimming. Choose a lane." Greta wanders to the end of the pool, pushing and pulling us into order.

We line up. The unknown adult keeps count of Pablo's laps.

The swimmer in front of me enters the pool. Greta shouts "Go! Go! Go!" I always feel as if I am dropping into a war zone when I enter the pool.

I dive. And swim. Water goes in my ears, my nose, my mouth, my goggles. The kid in front of me is too slow. I hit his heels. The kid behind me is too fast. He hits me. I stroke, breathe. Reach the end of the pool. Do it back again. And again. Which is the problem for me in swimming. I just don't get the action. It just seems like a lot of back and forth.

Practice ends. Pablo's swim ends. Bella and Mugsy pull him out of the pool to cheers all around. "Go, Pablo" fills the air. Coach Greta takes his picture as Pablo puts his arms around Sam the Man.

"Ten swimmers have shaken Sam's hand!" Coach Greta announces. "But that's not enough. I need more, more, more. If we want to raise the most money, we've got to try harder. Then we can beat the Sylvan Glen Sharks!" she promises. "And I'm not just talking about tomorrow's swim meet."

"But we never beat the Sharks," Timmy points out.

"They are all very, very big," Mad Dog adds.

"Rubbish!" she shouts. "You can beat them. Come on swimmers, say it with me." Coach Greta waves her arms from side to side, a kind of weird hula. "Go, Octopi. Go, Octopi."

Most of us stare at her. Except Timmy. He gets into it. Goes right up alongside her. Shaking his hips, he chants "Go, Octopi."

Jack calls out, "Towel hula!"

Before he can join the dance, the unknown lady with the clipboard says, "Ahem." Says it loudly, with a cough at the end.

Ahem?

"Oh, almost forgot you there, sport." Coach Greta pulls her to the front. "Swimmers, meet our new assistant, Coach Monsoon. She studies sports at college." Greta gives her a big thumbs-up there. "She does some work on, I don't know, children and sports. Isn't that exciting?" Coach Greta asks.

No one answers.

With an elbow to the stomach, Coach Greta reminds Assistant Coach Pablo that it's exciting.

"Exciting," says Pablo, nodding his dripping head up and down.

"Why is it exciting?" my little sister, Bella, wants to know.

"Why don't we call you by your first name, like the other coaches?" her friend Mugsy asks.

"Do you like turtles?" Mugsy's little brother, Mikey, asks.

"Greetings, swimmers," Coach Monsoon says, smiling a big, wide smile at all of us. "I am so happy to be here. So happy to answer your wonderful questions. Questions are such an important part of life. And sports are such an important part of life. So questions and sports together are, are . . ."

She seems to need help. "Such an important part of life?" I suggest.

"Exactly." She smiles at us again, as if we are the most wonderful kids she has ever met. Why, I don't know. She holds the smile and nods her head. A lot.

"You *are* using my first name. My name is Monsoon, Monsoon Mondshine. And I do like turtles, very much. Turtles are a part of this whole wide, wonderful world, which we live in together, as we share, as we grow."

She throws her arms wide. With each word, they go higher. And higher. Till they are up over her head, pointing to the sky.

"Holy moly, she's going to sing," Timmy swears.

Her hands to the sky, Coach Monsoon stares

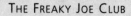

upward for a moment. We stare at her.

"Okay. Great intro-duction, Monsoon. Sure are having an exciting morning, aren't we?" Coach Greta steps in. "Remember Spirit Night starts at five o'clock." Greta rubs her hands together. "And tomorrow, the swim meet against the Sylvan Glen Sharks."

Great moans all around.

"We can beat the Sharks," our head coach cries. "Now, go forth and get sponsors."

Pablo calls out, "See you dudes later."

Coach Monsoon bows to us as we leave.

Bows?

Chapter Three

You Gotta Jump Down, Turn Around

"Okay, what is with that new coach?" Jack asks. "Coach Hurricane?"

"Monsoon," I tell him. "Her name is Coach Monsoon."

"Her name is Coach Weird," Jack insists.

"I thought she was going to start singing," Timmy repeats as he drips on the floor of The Secret Place. "Like opera, or something." He throws his arms wide and his mouth wider. "Sshhaarrkkss aandd tturrttlless."

Riley joins in.

So does Jack. "Sswwiimm iinn tthhee sseeaa."

Riley is the best singer.

I unlock the Book. Check again the secret information. They'll be finished soon.

"Okay." Jack snaps his fingers. "What do we have to do? Why are we having a meeting? I have to go work on my sponsor list." Jack heads toward the door. "I plan to call all the teachers at our school."

"Today's meeting is about Rule Seventeen D." I pause. "The secret signs." This stops Jack in his tracks.

"I am going to be so good at this," he declares. "I am so good at secrets."

Yes, and Riley is going to be the first opera-singing dog.

"Why do we need the signs?" Timmy asks. He finds something that survived swim team practice. So he has a little snack.

"So we are able to talk to each other, without talking. Which can be useful around bad guys. And I think we should take a break from using our code names. People are becoming suspicious." I could point out that this is due to the fact that certain members of our club yell code names in public. But I do not.

Freaky Joe's Rule Number Two C: The Club Leader Must Be Wise and Fair.

"What if You Know Who, the last bad guy, is the only villain we ever meet?" Timmy wonders.

"Yeah," Jack says. "Do you think we'll ever have another case?"

"I do," I answer. I *hope* is what I mean.

"Here's the first secret sign." I raise my arm straight up in the air and bend my wrist back and forth, making a goofy wave. "This means *go away*."

"It looks like *hello*," Jack notices.

"Exactly," I say.

"Aha," says Timmy.

"Huh?" says Jack.

"Secret signs are supposed to confuse people. Everyone but the people who know them. This is what makes them secret," I point out.

"Aha," says Jack.

"Doing this"—I hold my hands out to the side, like airplane wings and move them just a little—"means *come here*. If you add this"—my hands hold tight to a small,

shaking invisible steering wheel—"it means *come quick*."

"Jet airplane," Timmy sees.

"Aha," Jack says again.

24

I cover one eye with one hand.
"*Bad guy nearby.*" I move my
hand to the other eye. "And this
means *bad guy on this side.*"

"But what if they're behind
me?" Jack worries. "I don't have
an eye in the back of my head."

"You were listening in science
class, weren't you, Jack?"
Timmy examines Jack's
head. "You're right, you
only have two eyes."

"But I have one brain, and
that's one more than you," Jack
answers.

"Lame joke," Timmy comes back.

"Freaky Joe Club!" I shout.

"Sorry," Timmy says.

"I have a great idea," Jack says.

This is always a worry.

"Each one of us carries a fake eyeball at all times. If the bad guys are in front of us, we hold it up to our forehead."

"Fake eyeball?" I repeat. "At all times?"

"Am I the best at this, or what?" Jack asks.

"Or what," I answer.

Timmy jumps from one foot to the other, covering his eye with one hand. "Okay, I'm speaking in code. What am I saying?" Jack copies him. "What? What are we saying?"

"There is a bad guy on the right and I have to go to the bathroom," Timmy decodes.

Somehow I do not think he is taking this seriously. I put both my arms straight up in the air and flex my wrists back and forth.

"Uh-oh, Condor is talking in code," Jack notices.

"*The* Condor," Timmy corrects.

"Oh, oh, The Condor is talking in code," Jack repeats.

"He says," Timmy squints his eyes. "He says 'Touchdown!' Yes." Timmy begins his famous touchdown dance.

"That's not much of a secret, Conor," Jack points out.

"Because that's not what it means," I answer. "It means *Help*."

"Got it." Timmy signals for help.

"But what if we are surrounded by bad guys on all sides?" Jack looks like he really hopes this happens. "I would need to say 'Help,' and I would need to say 'Bad Guy This Way.' So I would need two extra eyeballs."

"And four extra hands." Timmy is in his help-ful mode.

"Right, six hands." Jack counts on his fingers.

"You show us how to do it, Jack," Timmy suggests.

Jack gives it a try.

Riley begins to howl.

"Someone's coming." Riley always lets me know.

"Or she wants Jack to stop that, now," Timmy suggests.

"What is Jack doing?" Bella asks as she sticks her head in the door.

"Nothing," Jack answers.

"It's a very funny nothing." Bella can see.

"He is not coming in here without knocking," I explain.

"Mommy says to tell you that she needs you." Bella ignores the No Knocking point. "You have to come help her paint the banner. And Mugsy and Mikey and me are your helpers."

Jack heads out the door at mach speed. "I gotta go work on my sponsors."

"Is your mom making lunch?" Timmy asks Bella as they leave.

I put both hands up straight in the air.

And I do not mean touchdown.

Chapter Four

Sing, Sing a Song

Spirit Night is in full swing at the Ship's Cove swimming pool. My mom and I hang a banner on the fence inside the pool. The other banner.

"Bella, just stand there in

the middle. Do not dance, or do cartwheels, or wave at your friends. Just stand," my mother explains.

Bella is helping us.

"Conor, is the banner straight?" Mom is trying to tie, lean back, make sure the banner is straight, and keep Bella from escaping all at the same time.

"I can't see. If I let go it'll fall." As I am plastered against the fence holding it, this would seem clear to me. But I am not an adult.

"Looking good, Mrs. M.," Coach Greta shouts from the other side.

"Straight?" shouts my mom.

"Big thumbs-up on that one." Greta gives her the sign.

After my mom tapes the corner above my head, I can stand back and look.

Large letters spell SQUISH THE FISH. A giant

octopus sits on a really scared-looking shark, wrapping his tentacles all around its head. Each tentacle has a boxing glove that whomps the shark.

My mom did the letters and the picture. It is easy to tell which part the rest of them did. Bella is now mostly pink, Mugsy a lovely shade of blue, and Mikey is mostly turtle green.

My mom is waiting for Bubba to come help her hang banner number one on the wall outside. That one says **WELCOME SYLVAN GLEN SHARKS.**

We give the other teams a friendly welcome. Outside the pool.

"I hope Mr. Butowski gets here soon." My mother scans the pool. As if she might miss seeing Bubba. "He's bringing the tall ladder."

Coach Monsoon drifts over to us. "You are the wonderful boy who spoke this morning. So nice to see you again. And are you this wonderful boy's mother?"

Coach Monsoon puts out her hand. At least she isn't bowing.

"And what wonderful person are you?" my mother asks.

"Mom, this is our new coach, Coach Monsoon," I explain. "She is studying sports at college."

"How interesting. Which college?"

"Did you make this sign?" Coach Monsoon asks.

"I did, with the kids," my mom explains. "It's a fun tradition we have here."

Coach Monsoon steps back to read it. And looks as if she just ate a dis-gusting jellybean from Timmy's backpack.

"But this is mean. And unsportsman-like. And unkind to fish." Coach

Monsoon has her hand to her mouth.

"Well, only unkind to sharks," I point out.

"It's called a joke," my mom says.

My mom is interrupted by the noise. Bubba arrives. Our ace security guard who loves dogs. Flowers. And some people. And the Ship's Cove swim team. He has on his special Support the Team outfit.

"Bubba. Bubba," the kids yell.

Bubba waves from the stairs. On his head, he wears an old-fashioned kind of ladies' swim cap. His long ponytail hangs out the back. On his face are purple swim goggles with a lighthouse on each side, and around his middle is a tube with a sea horse head on it. Perhaps Coach Monsoon would think it was mean, but I think it would be true, to say it is not a small middle.

"Ready to go, Riley's Mom?" he calls from across the pool.

"Coming, Mr. Butowski." Taking the banner, my mom heads Bubba's way.

"It must be hard for you," Coach Monsoon says.

Huh?

Before I can ask her "Huh?" she gets all excited again. "Look! What is that boy doing?"

At the other end of the pool, Jack points at me. Points and flaps. Runs in a circle. Moves his arms up and down like some giant bird. A giant, clumsy bird.

"He's pretending to be a seagull," I explain. "He love seagulls."

Jack is clearly speaking code to me. He flaps

with all his might. I have no idea what he is saying.

Coach Monsoon gets going. Again. "What a wonderful boy. He is communing with nature. I love nature." She does that Hands up to the Sky thing.

Which makes Jack leap into the water. "I'm coming!" he yells. Unfortunately he yells at the same time he tries to breathe. Which gives him a mouthful of water. He sputters. Tries to talk.

"Code word *Help!*" he points at Coach Monsoon.

Aha.

The lifeguards think Jack is calling for help. They blow whistles, leap into the water, save Jack.

Coach Greta blows her whistle because everyone else is.

More kids jump into the pool, which turns lovely blues, pinks, and greens near Bella, Mugsy, and Mikey.

"A lot of spirit here tonight," Timmy observes.

• • • •

After Jack's rescue, the Freaky Joe Club sits in one corner of the pool.

"Didn't you see me telling you to come here?" Jack whispers.

"No, I saw you imitating a large clumsy bird," I whisper back. "Airplanes do not flap their wings."

"Some do," Jack insists.

"None do," Timmy comes back.

"The important thing is, why did you want me to come over?" I try to remember that a Freaky Joe leader must be wise and kind.

My mom interrupts. "Are you okay, Jack?"

"Sharks!" Jack announces. "I saw Sharks."

"Where?" Timmy jumps back from the pool.

"Here?" my mom looks surprised.

"Not sharks." Jack sounds frustrated. "Sharks. Look!"

Three guys come into the pool. Three big guys.

"It's Jeremiah," I say.

"And Jake," Timmy sees.

"And Mick," Jack adds.

Three members of the Sylvan Glen Sharks walk across the pool to Coach Greta.

And I swear the water in the baby pool begins to move. Thud. Thud.

"I don't know those boys," my mom admits.

"They're from Sylvan Glen," I tell her.

"They swim on the Sharks," Jack says.

"And they go to our school," Timmy adds.

"They're big boys," Mom observes.

"They're our age," I admit.

"What do they feed them in Sylvan Glen?" my mother wonders. "Raw meat?"

"Does it taste good?" Timmy wants to know.

"I'm going to check on Bella." My mom wanders off.

The three Sharks hand Coach Greta some papers. Jeremiah keeps looking our way. Pointing with two hands.

"I'm not sure what he means by that," I say.

"Whatever it is," Timmy starts.

"It ain't good," Jack finishes.

Coach Pablo comes by. "Come on, dudes, line up at the end of the pool. It's picture time."

"But not song time?" I hope.

"Gotta sing the song, dude. Tradition." Pablo goes around gathering up swimmers. Coach Monsoon does the same. Coach Greta talks to the Sharks.

"Come on, cozy, cozy, cozy." Mad Dog's mother, the one who named him Charley, always takes the team picture. We squish each other, not the fish. And smile for the camera.

"Octopi!" Coach Greta shouts at us. "These nice boys from Sylvan Glen brought me a note from their coach."

The nice boys gesture behind her back. Not nice boy gestures.

"Mostly it is important and technical stuff we coaches understand. But it also brings news. They are two swimmers ahead of us in giving Sam a hand!" Greta looks shocked.

I'm pretty sure she is shocked that they are ahead. I am shocked they are ahead by so little. Winning is important in Sylvan Glen. The last swim meet they beat us by one hundred points.

"They may have had more swimmers than us. But remember our new motto: It's not the number of swimmers, but the number of sponsors." Coach Greta gives us one of those big We Share a Secret winks. "And we can send these boys back to Sylvan Glen with a little news. After tonight they're only ahead by one. Tonight, Coach Greta swims." She makes big muscles with both arms.

"She looks like Popeye," Timmy notices. Exactly like.

The Sharks look up from the banner they have been studying carefully. And appear impressed.

"She's scared them," Jack notices.

"Yeah, but they're not swimming against her," I remind them.

"True," Timmy notes.

"Monsoon, hey, skipper, would you and Pablo go get Sam?" Greta asks. "And remember, kids, the more sponsors, the more money. And more money means?" Greta puts her hands to her ear, waiting for our answer.

"How Much Water!" Mad Dog answers her.

"I'll never get ten sponsors," I whisper to Timmy. "I've only got one."

"Quiet now. Let's show these Sharks our team spirit." Coach Greta raises her arms like a conductor. I can't believe we are going to sing in front of them.

"One. Two. Three. Sing," Coach Greta orders.

We all sing. Some loudly.

"Octopi, my own Octopi,

We swim fast, oh yes, we fly.

Octopi, oh, Octopi,

Past us, you can't get by.

We have no legs, but lots of arms.

In the murky deep, we'll do you harm.

Octopi, yes, Octopi,

We won't win unless we try."

Some sing fast. Some slow. No one finishes at the same time. The three Sharks look like they are going to hurt themselves from laughing. Coach Greta looks delighted.

She wrote the song. As my mother says, who knew Coach Greta had "murky deep" inside her.

Our coach wipes her eye. "Swell, kids, just swell. And now it is Greta Swim Time."

"See ya," calls Jeremiah.

"Gotta go, gotta go," echo Jake and Mick.

The Sharks seem in a hurry to leave.

"See you tomorrow night, boys," Coach Greta calls to their backs as they hurry from the pool. "And swimmers, I have only one thing to say to you before tomorrow's meet, and that is . . ."

The two assistant coaches rush up. Alone. No flat dead Texas hero.

"Sam's gone!" Monsoon shouts.

"Nobody moves!"

Chapter Five

Where, Oh Where Has Our Little Sam Gone?

Nobody moves.

"He has to be there. Are you sure you checked?" Greta asks one of those adult questions.

"It's very difficult to overlook a life-size cutout of an important historical figure," Coach Monsoon explains.

She has a point there.

"This is no time to show you got smarts, Champ. I'm just asking if you really looked?"

"We looked," Pablo declares.

"Where could he be?" Coach Greta runs to the swim team storage closet.

Nobody moves.

Runs back out. "Sam Houston is missing!"

Which we already knew.

"Is this someone's idea of a joke?" Greta narrows her eyes, staring at each of us. Like she has X-ray vision, and can see where we hid Sam.

How could one of us take him? I mean, we're standing here in our bathing suits. And swim team boys' bathing suits are not the biggest. You can't put anything in them. Well, Timmy manages to. But no one else. And even he couldn't hide a piece of cardboard bigger than all of us.

"I'm sure there is an explanation for this." My mother does the adult thing now. "Where was it when you last saw it?"

"That would be where I just looked!" Greta explains.

"When was the last time anyone saw Sam?" Mom wants the facts. Freaky Joe's Rule Number Eight: Facts Are Important.

"I saw him when we got here," I report. "When I went to the closet to get the tape."

Greta doesn't seem interested in those facts. "Who would take our Sam?" she yells.

"The Sharks would," Jack answers.

The air fills with the sound of Octopi voices.

Saying "Yeah!"

And "Sharks!"

"We need Sam to swim, don't we?" Mugsy asks.

More "Yeah!"

And "Sharks!"

Greta wheels around.

"They're getting away," Mad Dog shouts.

Greta bolts for the gate.

Coach Pablo follows.

Coach Monsoon wrings her hands.

"Can we move now?" I ask.

"Of course you can move." Coach Monsoon waves her hands at us.

Like she is shooing some dog away. "Oh, what if Greta catches those boys? She is too angry for such a small thing."

"If she catches them, they're goners." It's Jack's turn to be helpful.

Coach Monsoon moans.

"I know, I'll call Mr. Butowski." My mother grabs her phone.

"Tell him they stole Coach Greta's dog," Timmy suggests.

"What?" asks my mother.

"A dog," I explain. "Tell Bubba some boys from Sylvan Glen are kidnapping a Ship's Cove dog. That way he'll chase them."

My mother looks at me as if I have two heads. But only for a moment. Pushing the buttons she says, "Very good idea."

Coach Greta and Pablo return. Out of breath and without Sam.

"I almost caught them, I swear," Greta huffs.

Pablo's face is a funny shade of purple. It's a little hard to follow his words. "She almost—*gasp, gasp*—caught up with those—*gasp, gasp*—kids on bicycles."

"Whoa, that would be a major land-speed record." Jack is impressed. Fingers are snapping.

Timmy fishes something that looks like it once was a lollipop out of his bathing suit.

That would be a bathing suit without pockets.

"Would you like this?" He offers it to Coach Greta.

"Thanks, sport." Greta pops it into her mouth. "I'm hoping Butowski will find them."

Pablo worries. "We never lost sight of them the whole way. They were definitely not carrying Sam."

We all wait a little longer till Bubba shows up. He wears the swim cap and goggles. But no sea horse tube.

"I talked to those boys," he reports, "but they didn't know anything about a pool toy. And they weren't carrying anything big."

Coach Greta almost swallows the lollipop. "We are not looking for a pool toy! We are looking for Sam Houston."

Bubba looks worried. "I don't think I know that dog."

A little while later, we parade through the back gate. My mom, Bella, Mugsy, Mikey, Timmy, Jack, and Mad Dog and his mother, who named him Charley and likes to take pictures. Even Coach Monsoon walks with us.

"This evening is not a good evening. The world, the wonderful, natural world feels wrong. I would like to walk with my fellow humankind as I go to my car," she says.

A terrible noise greets us.

"What is that terrible noise?" Coach Monsoon looks like she is about to jump out of her wonderful, natural skin.

"That's Riley," Timmy says, taking a different lollipop out of his mouth to tell her. I do not want to know where that one came from.

"Be very brave," Jack warns Coach Monsoon.

"She just wants to play," Timmy promises.

"Bella, do not open the door," my mom orders. At least I think that's what she says. She juggles towels, pool toys, tape, string, and a cell phone, and carries her keys in her mouth. It is a little hard to understand her.

Maybe I should be carrying something besides my towel.

Bella opens the door.

Riley explodes into the yard. So happy. She runs around in those big doggy circles. Stops by, now and again, to throw herself up on someone with a big kiss.

Coach Monsoon tries to run. She heads around the back of The Secret Place.

"There's no way out there," I tell her. There's just a sliver of wall between the side of The Secret Place and the fence.

"She tries to eat my flesh," Jack warns her.

"I am not afraid of dogs." Coach Monsoon's voice quivers.

"Conor, grab that beast," my mom insists. "I don't want her to escape."

"But Bubba will bring her home," Bella reminds her.

"And then Riley will be plump," Jack says.

"Monsoon, you can't go out that way." My mom sees her going the wrong way to behind the garage. "Don't worry about the dog."

"She only wants to eat Jack's flesh," Timmy assures her. "Here you go, girl." Timmy corrals her with his lollipop.

"I am not afraid of dogs," Coach Monsoon insists. "They are part of the world, the whole, lovely . . ."

"World." My mom finishes for her. "A lovely world. And a lovely, exciting night. And all good things must come to an end.

Peggy and Mad Dog will see you to your lovely car."

"I named him Charley," Peggy interrupts.

"Peggy and Mad Dog, who was named Charley, will see you to your lovely car on this lovely street, a small corner of the lovely universe."

I look at this adult person waving bye-bye. And wonder, *What have the aliens done with my real mother?*

Chapter Six

What Was That She Said?

"Am I lovely too?" Bella asks my mom.

"No. You are extraordinary," she tells Bella. "Extraordinary and late for bed." My mother issues orders. "Into the house, everyone who lives in this wonderful, natural world."

"Mom, we just have to stop in The Secret Place. Just for one sec. Jack left his sponsor list there."

"No I did—ow!" I use a secret sign to stop Jack. I step hard on his foot.

"For a nanosecond. A lovely nanosecond." My mom sings to Bella, "You are so lovely," as they dance into the house.

"Our second case begins!" I announce. "Let's make a quick plan." This is great.

"Plan?" Jack asks.

"For solving the crime. The Freaky Joe Club rides again."

"But we know who did it," Jack insists.

"Which makes it not so big a mystery," Timmy adds.

"Did the Sharks have Sam?" I ask.

"Big no," says Timmy.

"Did the Sharks tell Bubba where they put it?"

"They were probably too busy laughing at the swim hat," Jack thinks.

"They probably ditched it," Timmy says.

"Wouldn't Greta have found it?"

"Big yes," Timmy agrees.

"Did the Sharks take Sam? Mystery Number One." I hold up one finger to make it simple. "If the Sharks took him, where is he? Mystery Number Two."

Timmy holds up two fingers.

"And, if they didn't take him, who did? Mystery Number Three. Any way you count it, we have ourselves a case."

"So what's next?" Jack asks.

"I'm ready." Timmy salutes.

"We wait till tomorrow morning. First thing after swim team practice, we ride!"

"Ride where?" my fellow detectives wonder.

"Into the heart of enemy territory," I answer.

"Conor, we're going to be there too early," Bella insists as we walk out the gate to swim practice.

"No, we're a little bit late. We should hurry."

"No, it's too early," she insists.

"A little bit late."

"See?" she says as we get to the gate. "I was right."

"See what?" I ask.

"It's too quiet. We're too early."

I see. Inside the gate there's almost no noise.

"Come on." I grab her hand as we rush inside.

Swimmers hang around at the end of the pool. Some jump off the diving board, which is closed. Timmy and Jack flick wet towels at Mad Dog and his buddy Brendan.

No one yells at them. No one blows a whistle.

"What happened to Coach Greta?" I ask Timmy.

"There she is." Bella points.

Greta sits in a chair. Humming. Twirling her whistle around one finger. And off. And back again. It goes nowhere near her mouth.

"Strange, eh?" Timmy says. "She's like one of those creepy movies. You know, when it goes really quiet?"

"But you just know the scary guy is hiding in the bushes," Jack continues.

"I don't think Bella should be hearing this." I cover her ears.

"No, this is a game Mugsy plays all the time," she says. "Now you have to go 'Whooooo,' like a ghost."

Timmy goes "Whooooo."

"The guy who is going to get it keeps walking, even though it is too quiet," Jack says.

Bella does this great arm swinging, whistling, No Worries for Me walk.

I have got to talk to my mom about Mugsy's games.

"Then this really bad guy jumps out of the bushes." Jack does a move which could be bad guy or could be orangutan imitation. "He's wearing a football helmet, and waving an electric scissors."

"Football helmet?" Bella asks.

"Electric scissors?" I just gotta ask.

"Something like that." Details have never been very important to Jack.

"Would electric scissors be big enough to chop someone up?" Timmy wonders.

"The point is." Jack stops pretending to be a large crazy man or ape. "The point is . . ."

"It's too quiet," I finish for him.

"Right."

Pablo tells Coach Greta, "I'm sure we can get another sign."

"Who cares?" Greta twirls. And twirls.

"Yes, what does it matter?" Coach Monsoon tries to help. "Today is a beautiful day. Look, clouds float. Birds sing. The wonderful children are here. A silly piece of cardboard of a man no one cares about is not important."

Coach Greta stands up. Slowly. "Monsoon," she says. Slowly. "You can take that idea and . . ."

WHEW! WHEW! WHEW! Pablo has grabbed

the whistle and is blowing with all his might.

"Okay dudes, everyone in the pool. Go. Go. Go."

We dive, dive, dive. But some of us heard what Greta said. Our teacher, Mrs. Staley, would call those Describing Words.

A short while later, the secret agents of the Freaky Joe Club head out on a patrol. Dripping, but ready for action.

"Do we take notes this time?" Jack asks.

"Your choice. The important thing is to keep your eyes peeled for General Sam Houston." I imagine him riding a horse up Ahoy Mates Boulevard. He's wearing his Cherokee clothes, shouting "Here I am!" That might even take Bubba's attention away from a dog.

"Which way we heading?" Timmy wants to know.

"Let's take the back way into Sylvan Glen, okay?"

"The last time we did that, that funny lady threw candy corn at us," Jack remembers.

"She only does that at Halloween." I think.

"It was good candy corn," Timmy remembers.

"It was at Easter," Jack points out.

"That's an Easter tradition in small countries in the Carpathian Mountains," I tell him. "We're safe today."

"Too bad," says Timmy.

"What book did you read that in?" Jack asks.

I don't want to bother going through the front gate of Sylvan Glen. They have one security guard who sits by the front gate in a little house shaped like a log cabin. There are fake deer around the cabin, and fake squirrels running across the roof. Fake ducks swim in a fake pool. And there's a fake moose. We may not have *much* water in Ship's Cove, but there *is* water in the state of Texas. There are no moose.

The guard always wants to know who you are

visiting, and whether they know you are coming. Once he asked me for the license number of my bicycle.

I do not want to have to explain a missing cardboard Sam Houston. It's easier to risk a candy corn bruise.

We fly down Peg Leg Way and turn into Land Ho Lane. As we ride down, Smidgen wanders toward us. All alone.

"Smidgen has a new 'do,'" Timmy notices.

"And it's weirder than the last one," Jack says.

Smidgen, a teeny tiny dog, has a nice owner who doesn't throw things at children. But she does get Smidgen very strange haircuts.

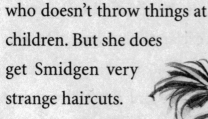

"Look, his hair bows match his nail polish." Timmy stops to pet him.

"This is a nice dog," Jack says. "See, he isn't trying to eat me, are you, strange little dog." Jack leans over to pet him. Smidgen growls and bares his teeth. "Whoa, evil midget," Jack yells.

"What should we do with him?" Timmy asks.

"Let's wait a minute. I want to ask Bubba to help us anyway." Two minutes later Bubba shows up.

"Smidgen. Are you trying to scare your mommy and Uncle Bubba?"

The dog is smaller than one of Bubba's hands. He sits in one, happily eating a treat.

"Poor thing, he must be terrified to be so far from home," Bubba exclaims. Smidgen, who was fine, starts to shake.

"Thanks for helping, boys. I don't know how he got out." Bubba uses his big finger to scratch the dog's little head.

I know how he got out. He ran away. Cut a screen, tied sheets together, slid down, and ran.

Looking for Bubba and his rolling Dog
Treats. We have a whole neighborhood of
runaway animals. Dogs Gone Bad. And
it is all Bubba's fault.

"Did you find your pool toy yet?"
Bubba asks.

"It is not a pool toy, Bubba,"
Timmy tries to explain. "It
is more important than
that."

"We have to find it," Jack swears.

I act on Freaky Joe's Rule Number
Nineteen: Any Help Is Good Help.

"Bubba," I begin, "Sam Houston was a
great man in Texas."

"Of course he was." Bubba knows. "He
built our city."

"More than that, Mr. Butowski," I go on. "Sam
Houston was the first president of Texas. And
the man who said every Texan has a right to

own a dog. He made stealing a dog a hanging offense."

"Makes you proud, doesn't it?" Bubba Butowski puts his hand over his heart. Which crushes Smidgen. "It just makes a man so proud."

"Someone took our Sam, Bubba. And Coach Greta is so sad. We've just gotta get him back."

"Bubba is on the job." He salutes as he drives off. "I'll take this little rascal home, and find that president pool toy."

"Where did you learn that about Sam Houston?" Jack asks as we ride on.

"Do you know you might be an evil genius?" Timmy says.

"Why?" asks Jack.

"There's the hole in the wall," I point. At the end of Land Ho Lane, a break in the stone wall leads from Ship's Cove into Sylvan Glen.

I feel like Remington Reedmarsh as he heads toward the Great Battle against the Tyrant Tyler. For I know that my cause is just. And that my enemy is Very Large.

Chapter Seven

Earth to Jack, Earth to Jack

The green trees of Sylvan Glen overhang the path as we wend our way through the beautiful forest. It's a place filled with curious, large, candy-tossing creatures. Who can swim fast.

We ride up Lovely Lilac Lane. Timmy calls out "Here, Sammy, Sammy. Here, Sammy, Sammy." Which doesn't seem to work. He switches to "Here, candy, candy. Here, candy, candy." With the same result.

Spying no one made of cardboard, we ride to Pretty Penny Park.

"What's the plan?" Timmy wants to know.

"Can we feed those ducks?" Jack asks.

Pretty Penny Park has real water, with real

ducks. Real pretty white park benches. All lovely. Coach Monsoon would love this beautiful natural world. But she couldn't use it because she doesn't live here.

"We can't feed ducks, Jack. We are looking for clues. Anything that will help solve the mystery."

"Anything?" Jack asks.

"How about three large guys who were there when Sam went missing?" Timmy asks.

"That would be good," I guess.

"Because here they come," Timmy points out.

I look up to see Jeremiah, Jake, and Mick speeding down on us.

"This is good?" Jack asks.

"Octopi. Oh, Octopi." The three Shark boys make a circle around us. Singing our own theme song. Worse than we do. Which is hard.

But maybe this is not the time to tell them.

"You guys got such a nice so-ong," Jake says in what I am sure would be called a sneer.

"Thanks a lot," I reply ever-so-politely. "We like it."

This is clearly not the answer Jake expected. He actually scratches his head.

"So, did you guys come over here to get us in more trouble?" Jeremiah asks. He rocks his bike back and forth, like he is going to roll over us. This would actually be scary if his bicycle had a motor. Still, it is a big bicycle. And he's a big guy.

"No," I answer honestly. "We didn't come over here to get you in trouble. Timmy, did we come to get these guys in trouble?" I have always found that Polite is a good strategy.

"No, I was looking for candy corn," Timmy answers truthfully.

"You told your mondo weirdo security guard that we stole something from your pool." Mick pounds one fist into another.

"No, I never said that." I don't know any mondo weirdo security guard. Maybe weirdo, but not mondo. So I am technically truthful.

"What's wrong with him?" Jeremiah wants to know.

Jack is busy putting his hand on one eye. And then the other. He moves it to the back of his head. And the front of his head. This is so useful. We would never have guessed there are bad guys around.

"He is sick," I answer.

"It makes him happy," Timmy says at the exact same time.

"Huh?" Jake asks.

A clue. There is a clue here. I can tell.

"Happy, because he is sick," I explain. "He has terrible pain and he feels better if he does this."

"That is so funny I forgot to laugh," Jake says.

"You looking to start a fight?" Mick asks with more fist slapping.

Aha! Now I see.

"No, I don't think so." I think seriously for a moment. My hand to my chin. "No, we don't want to start a fight."

"No," Timmy agrees.

Jack signals away that there are bad guys nearby.

"So you are snooping?" Jeremiah asks. "What are you looking for?"

"A life-size cutout of Sam Houston," I report.

"We only have ours and you better not take it," he threatens.

"We want ours, not yours," I answer.

"Well, we don't have it," Jeremiah answers.

"No, you don't," I reply. "I know." Because I do. And we have to go.

With this new information it is time to return to The Secret Place.

"Are you trying to be funny?" Jeremiah curls both hands into fists.

Jack puts both hands up into the air.

"Touchdown!" Jake yells.

"Why is he doing that?" Mick asks.

"There is something funny going on around here," Jeremiah notices.

"Where's the football?" asks Jake.

"Well, we need to go now," I tell the Sharks.

"Because Jack is sick," Timmy reminds them.

"Timmy," I call. My hands grip a small,

shaking-from-speed steering wheel.

"Gotcha, gotcha." He shakes Jack. "Come on, boy. We need a land-speed record."

Jack's fingers snap. "I can beat anyone," he says automatically.

"You guys are like so completely weird," Jeremiah declares.

"Mondo weird," Mick agrees.

"Are we playing football?" Jake asks.

"Mondo gone," I declare.

We ride.

My mind turns as fast as the pedals. With this new information, the case becomes much clearer. And much more difficult.

Chapter Eight

Black Widows, Smart Sharks?

Back in Ship's Cove, we slow our pace. Passing Mugsy's house, I see Bella and Mugsy hanging upside down from a tree. Mikey and a friend sit on the ground. They have something attached to their heads.

"You know you're not supposed to hang

upside down to make yourself sick." One of the best things about adopting Bella is that I get to do this big brother stuff.

"Does it work?" Jack asks.

"We're not doing that," Bella insists.

"We're being black widow spiders," Mugsy tells us.

"And Mikey and Dwayne are going to fly into our web," Bella says.

Mugsy makes a truly evil-looking face. And big chopping motions with her teeth.

The boys look terrified.

I really have to talk to my mom about Mugsy's games.

"Secret agents of the Freaky Joe Club, we have work to do," I announce as soon as we are safe in The Secret Place.

"Do you have an idea where the Sharks hid Sam?" Timmy wants to know. He settles into a beanbag chair, chewing one of Riley's bones.

I tape a big piece of paper to the wall. With a marker I write

IMPORTANT INFORMATION ABOUT THE CASE

and underneath I write

THE SHARKS DID NOT TAKE OUR SAM.

"What? I didn't hear them say that," Jack protests.

"You didn't hear anything but messages from that planet you were orbiting," Timmy informs him.

"I was speaking in secret code," Jacks says huffily.

"Speaking to the people of the Planet Zygphkt." Timmy turns into a space explorer. "Many-headed space people, I bring you greetings, and a large supply of candy corn."

"Yeah, well watch out, or I'll zap you with my death ray," Jack threatens.

They'll be done soon. I wait. And wonder why people and planets in outer space never have vowels in their names.

"But how do you know that, Conor? I didn't hear them say anything," Timmy admits.

"Even if they did steal it, they would say that they didn't. So how come you're so sure?" Jack works out the logic.

"Because if they had it they would have said," I do a good imitation of Jake's voice. "'We don't have your stupid Sam. Do we, guys?' And then he would look at the others, shaking his head.

"And they would have said, 'Oh no, we don't have it.' And they would do those goofy, We Know Something You Don't Know laughs. Then roll their eyes.

"They would say 'Take your Sam? Why would we do something like that?' And then they would laugh in some other stupid way." I pause for breath.

"Which would really make it seem like they did it." Jack sees my point.

"While they thought they were acting smart." Timmy gets it.

"Which these guys can't do," I remind them.

"But the point is"—I put stars around the sentence I wrote—"the Sharks did not take our Sam."

"Aha," Jack agrees.

"Now what?" Timmy asks.

"Now we have to go swim in a meet against the Sharks," Jack reminds us. "And lose badly."

"We still have to solve this case," I remind Jack.

"You know what I don't know?" Timmy admits. "Why would someone want to take him?"

Good question.

I have the feeling that there is something important I should see. But I don't.

After we argue about it, I write our ideas on a list:

WHY WOULD SOMEONE STEAL OUR SAM HOUSTON?

1) They want to decorate their house.
2) They are lonely and want company.
3) They are related to Sam Houston.
4) They hate all the Octopi.
5) They just hate Coach Greta.
6) They don't want to get sponsors and swim.

I look at the list, and I have that feeling again.

"Aha," says Jack.

"What?" I missed something that Jack sees?

"You did it." He points an accusing finger at me.

"What?" Now I know I missed something.

"Number six is the best reason," Timmy agrees. "And you keep saying you don't want to get ten sponsors."

"Tell us where he is," Jack tells me. "And we'll put him back."

"No one will know," Timmy promises.

"One problem," I want them to know.

"What?"

"I didn't take him."

"You sure?" Jack asks.

"Very sure," I promise.

"Could this be a test?" Timmy suggests. "We will be real and true detectives when we find out you did it. Then we get to look in the Freaky Joe Club book."

"That would be a good idea."

"Aha," says Jack.

"But I didn't do it."

"Aha," Jack says, I hope for the last time. "Your great-great-great-grandfather was Sam Houston. You want to stop the Give Sam a Hand contest."

"Not related," I promise. "We are down to someone who hates us, or Coach Greta." Stop the contest?

"What about One and Two? I think those are good ideas," Jack insists. Not to mention that those ideas were his ideas.

"Or maybe hates Greta's whistle," Timmy suggests.

"You don't like her whistle."

"Jack!"

"Okay, you didn't do it." Pause. "Do you hate Coach Greta, Conor?"

"Jack, I didn't do it."

"Just checking. So it has to be the Sharks," Jack decides.

"Who didn't do it," I remind him.

"But what if those Sharks didn't take him, but

other, smarter Sharks did?" Timmy asks.

"Ooh, Timmy has his thinking cap on." Jack answers.

"There's a good point," I say. Because it is.

"What are we going to do?" Jack paces and snaps. "It's almost time for the meet."

"We're going to have to talk to lots of Sharks," I think. "See if anyone gets that goofy I Know Something You Don't Know smile."

"Then we get 'em?" Timmy asks

"Can Sharks smile?" Jack asks.

"Think it will work?" Timmy asks.

"If we're going to talk to that many Sharks," Jack warns, "I'd better go get my extra eyeball."

I keep staring at the list. "You know, I feel as if I know something. But I don't know what it is I know."

"Don't worry," Jack says. "I feel like that all the time."

Chapter Nine

Who Played Knickknack on My Gate?

Good. Good. Balancing *The Big Book of Undersea Life*, I scribble notes on a small square of paper. And hope they are scribbles that someone else can read. The someone I scribble them for.

Riley begins to bark. "People coming," she informs me.

"Don't let her out." I look up to see Timmy, Bella, Mugsy, Mikey, and his little buddy Dwayne.

"I'm helping your mom by taking the kids to warm up," Timmy informs me.

"I'll be there in a sec. As soon as I finish this," I promise.

Timmy leads a parade of small Octopi out the

back gate, chanting all the way, "Sharks smile. Sharks smile."

Maybe I should change the name on our book to The Not-So-Secret Files of the Freaky Joe Club.

Riley barks and barks the news that more people are coming.

I finish the notes while I wait for Jack to barge in.

Riley keeps barking.

Very funny, Jack, I think. I open the back door. The back gate closes shut.

Riley barks again.

"Jack, cut it out," I call out. No answer.

I go inside. One more sentence and then I'm finished.

The Riley alarm goes off.

Mom must be on her way. I finish my notes.

Riley is going nuts.

I open the door. Again, the gate closes shut. Someone is on the other side.

"Very funny. I'm a lonely mad scientist with an ugly house who knew Sam Houston," I call out as I head to the gate. Someone runs away fast.

"Conor, could you come help me?" My mother carries all her usual stuff and a microphone.

"Why is Riley fussing so?" she wants to know.

"Jack is being goofy, opening and closing the back gate," I explain.

"How could he do that?" she says. "He just rode past our house. Odd. He covered one eye as he went. Who is he worried about?"

"Probably the Sharks," I explain. And I wonder: If Jack wasn't at the back gate, who was?

It is definitely not too quiet at the pool tonight. Swim meets are noisy. Coaches shout advice. Lifeguards shout "don't run." Kids run. Lifeguards yell "We still have pinecones in the pool." Whistles are blown. Swimmers splash and call out to Bubba as he wanders around in his outfit. Twelve kids dive in to clean up four pinecones. The announcer announces.

At least the announcer will in one moment. My mom is the Voice of the Octopi.

Right now the biggest noise comes from Mugsy and Bella. Howling. Mikey and Dwayne sob too. A crowd of Octopi surrounds them.

"What's wrong?" My mom gets there in two steps. Which must break the land-speed record at that distance. An important rule to remember is: Do not mess with Bella. Mom doesn't do well with that.

Neither do I.

The girls wail in front of the Squish the Fish banner—what used to be the Squish the Fish banner. The octopus and shark are gone. They've been cut out of the middle, with the sides hanging loose.

My mother stares, presses her lips together, puts her hands on her hips, and narrows her eyes.

"A Shark is going down tonight," Timmy says.

My mom puts her arms around both girls. "Don't cry, sweeties. It's just a banner. We can make another one."

"But now we won't have time to swim!" Bella sobs.

"Of course you'll have time to swim." My mother tries the voice of reason.

"No we won't, because now we have to destroy someone," Mugsy howls.

"Us too," Mikey and Dwayne wail.

I leave my mother to calm down the Six and Under Death Squad. Coach Pablo tries to organize the Octopi. Coach Monsoon heads out the gate, leaving the pool.

"I'll be right back," she calls. No one seems to be listening. She has a bundle under her arm.

Head Coach Greta sits shuffling heat sheets, which say who swims when.

"Excuse me," I interrupt her.

"Mad Dog's mom can tell you what race you're in," Greta says, answering a question I didn't ask.

"She named him Charley," I tell her.

"Whatever."

"Did you see the banner?" I ask.

"Whatever."

"Would you read this note?" I give her the piece of paper.

"Whatever."

"Thanks," I answer. This does not rank as the most exciting conversation I have ever had.

Coach Monsoon runs back in, empty handed. What did she leave outside? I wonder.

My mother's voice comes through the speakers. "All Ship's Cove Octopi come to the shallow end of the pool. All Sharks meet your coach by the diving board. Anyone who thinks ripping up other people's artwork is funny should report to the announcer's booth."

No one comes.

Jack walks over, holding Bella and Mugsy's hands. Actually, pulling them by the hand. Timmy carries Mikey under one arm and Dwayne under the other.

"You have to stop," Jack tells them as he pulls. "They keep running through the Sharks yelling 'Death to Banner Rippers,'" he tells me.

"It makes it hard to check the smile thing," Timmy lets me know.

"The meet will begin in five minutes," the announcer announces. "Don't forget to taste delicious food from the concession stand. Goggles and swim caps are for sale. Paper is available for anyone wishing to write an apology for destroying property."

"She's still angry," Jack notices.

The Sharks form a big circle around their coach.

He yells, "Who's the meanest fish in the sea?"

"The shark!" they answer.

"Who has the biggest teeth in the sea?" he asks.

"The shark!" they shout.

"Who uses them to tear flesh from his enemies' bones?"

"The shark!"

"And does the shark like to eat octopi?"

"He does! He does!"

"Let's go have a great meet," the coach says.

I am very glad no one on our team is bleeding right now. There would be a shark feeding frenzy.

The Octopi gather in a loose group.

"Don't worry about them, little dudes," Pablo urges. One or two of our swimmers visibly shake.

"What a way to speak to children! The world of the sea is a beautiful place." Coach Monsoon is horrified. Clearly she missed that Great White Shark television special.

"Does no one see what is happening?" she asks. "This is supposed to be swimming for fun. How can he say such things?"

"Because he doesn't know about Octopi!" Coach Greta pushes into the center of our huddle. "And because sharks have itty, bitty brains," she says in a very loud voice.

"Now, who are some of the smartest creatures in the sea?" Coach Greta calls out.

The swim team stares at her.

"Octopi!" I shout.

"They are?" Mad Dog asks.

"Who have the most complex brains of all," she checks her little piece of paper "of all . . ."

"Invertebrates!" I shout.

"Invertebrates being creatures without backbones!" Greta shouts as she reads.

"Octopi!" the team answers.

"Invertebrates, invertebrates!" they shout.

"And who have great long and short term memories?"

"Octopi!" the Octopi answer. "Long and short term memories!"

"Who can solve problems by both experience, and trial and error!"

"We can, we can!"

"You are gonna go out and swim," Greta tells us. "We are going to show the Sharks what complex-brained invertebrates can do!"

"Yeah! Yeah!"

"Let's start off with a bang. Six and under mixed relay front and center."

Coach Greta calls out the names. "Bella."

The team cheers. "Bella. Bella."

"Mugsy," Greta reads from her list. "And Mikey."

"Mugsy," they call. And "Turtle man! Turtle man!"

"And Dwayne. Let's go Octopi!"

Silence.

"Dwayne?" Jack wonders.

"We have to have two boys. Dwayne will do fine."

"The meet will start in two minutes," the announcer says.

Chapter Ten

The Silver Streak

"We're sunk," Jack declares.

"Maybe they'll hurt themselves laughing," Timmy suggests.

Dwayne stands there, all hangdog. He is the shortest kid on the team, the skinniest, the boniest. His bathing suit is too big. He holds it up with two hands at all times. Even when he dives—no, throws himself—into the pool, he holds his suit up.

He wears these goofy goggles that look like a Batman mask. They are way too big for him. And the goggles always come off halfway down the pool. Then Dwayne holds on to the rope, holds up his suit and tries to fix his goggles.

Wars have been fought and lost in the time it

takes Dwayne to get to the other end of the pool.

"Don't worry, Dwayne." Timmy pounds him on the back. "You can do this."

"Yeah, you just have to get to the other end of the pool," I encourage him.

"That is very, very, very far," Dwayne says.

"We're done," Jack says.

We need help. Dwayne needs help. And I know where to get it.

I send Jack to tell the announcer that the timer needs another minute. I send Timmy to tell the timer that the announcer needs another minute.

"Dwayne, follow me," I take him by the hand to the supply closet. Timmy and Jack follow.

• • • •

"First swimmers in place," the starter announces as we rush Dwayne up to take his place. He swims after Bella and Mikey, with Mugsy to finish.

"Swimmers, take your mark." The starter buzzes.

Bella hits the water. Goes fast to the other side. She and the Shark swimmer get there at almost the same time. Mikey swims back, not so fast, but he's coming.

"High five, Dwayne," I tell him. He hits me with two free hands. "Fast to the other side, buddy," I tell him. "No stopping."

"No stopping," Dwayne says. He glitters in the late afternoon sun. Duct tape holds his bathing suit to his body. Wrapped around and around. The goggles are going nowhere. They are taped to his head.

Mikey touches the wall.

"Go!" I shout. Dwayne flies out and into the sky, a silver streak as he hits the water.

Arms wild. Head bobbing up and down.

The crowd chants. "Dwayne! Dwayne! Dwayne!"

He seems to be moving all muscles in his body, but still staying in the same spot.

The Shark in the other lane moves on ahead. Dwayne inches forward.

I race across to the other side to be there when he finishes. "Dwayne, come here!" I scream. He seems to hear me. Gets going. A little.

The Shark next to Mugsy gets ready to go. "Eat my bubbles," she tells Mugsy, crouching into her dive.

Dwayne is coming, he's coming.

"See ya," the girl says to Mugsy, as her team-mate nears the wall.

"Oooh, what's that in the water?" Mugsy asks. "It's black and round and long."

"Where?" the girl Shark asks. Her teammate touches the wall. "What is it?" She stands up.

"I can't see," Mugsy says. "It looks gross."

"Eeewww!" the Shark swimmer cries.

"Go! Go!" her coach screams.

Dwayne keeps coming. The girl keeps looking down.

Her coach pushes her into the water.

Dwayne touches the wall. Mugsy flies out. The Shark begins swimming with all her might.

But she had a bad start.

Mugsy gets there first.

The pool explodes.

The Shark comes up screaming.

"Someone should get that pinecone out of the other end of the pool," Mugsy tells the ref. "But I did warn the other team."

We race the Sharks for hours. Jack, Timmy,

Mad Dog, and I swim faster then ever before. Jeremiah, Jake, Mick, and his brother Mike still win. But we come in second, not third.

Murphy, Mugsy's big sister, wins three races. Mugsy leads everyone in cheering, "Mugsy's sister! Mugsy's sister!"

Fifty races later, the meet ends. Both teams wait for the announcer.

Coach Monsoon wanders around asking, "Why do we need the score?"

We wait, holding our breath.

Then the voice over the loudspeaker.

"Although all scores may not be settled," Mom announces, "I have the final score. Sylvan Glen Sharks: 168. Ship's Cove Octopi: 152."

The Octopi stand without moving.

"See! See!" Monsoon says to the other coaches. "Look at these sad, sad children. This is what happens when sports are . . ."

No one hears the rest of her sentence. The Octopi explode. Jump into the air. Into the pool. Into the air. Scream. High five. Towel hula.

"Yes, ladies and gentlemen and swimmers of

all ages. The Sharks win by only sixteen points."
The announcer sounds very pleased.

I start a chant. "Sixteen points. Sixteen points."
The announcer joins in over the PA system.

"Why are people cheering? You lost. You are
crushed, and it is all the adults' fault." Confused
would describe Monsoon right now.

Into the pool goes Greta. And Pablo. Monsoon
almost. "I can't swim," she screams.

Mugsy and Bella start a conga line. Dancing to
the rhythm of "Invertebrates, invertebrates."

The thought that kept flying away from me
lands. I see. *Aha*, I think.

I have to talk to Jack and Timmy. Timmy, with
Dwayne on his shoulders, now leads the conga
line. Jack is not far behind. Everyone sings
"Dwayne has a complex brain."

I dance alongside. "We have to talk," I say
softly.

"What?" Timmy can't hear me. Jack either.

"I have to tell you something very, very important," I say louder.

Coach Greta grabs the mike. "This is a great day, Octopi," she declares. "Nothing could make this day better." Pause. "Okay, winning would be better. But that is all."

"Coach Greta," Bubba calls loudly as he struggles with the gate.

And makes her day even better.

Chapter Eleven

He Did It?

"Butowski!" Coach Greta zooms across the pool. Bubba and Sam Houston squeeze through the gate she holds open.

"Bubba found our Sam!" Greta yells to the Octopi. "Let's give him a cheer."

Sounds fills the air. "Yay," and "Hooray," and "Bubba," and a few times, "Invertebrate." Even though Bubba does have a backbone.

Bubba stands there with hat, goggles, swim tube, and Sam. And looking like he is not so happy about the cheering.

I can't believe he is going to get the credit for another case.

"That was the important thing you wanted to tell us?" Timmy realizes.

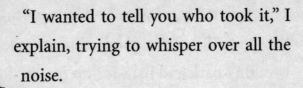

"I wanted to tell you who took it," I explain, trying to whisper over all the noise.

"Who did it?" they both ask me.

With one sweep of her arm, Greta silences the crowd. "Butowski, where did you find our Sam?"

Bubba looks down. He scuffs the toes of his shoes. "It's not important."

I wonder where he found it. The thief did not have much time to hide it. I know.

"Bubba." Greta has his arm in what looks like an uncomfortable grip. "Where did you find this?"

Bubba spills the beans. "I heard Riley barking.

This worried me, 'cause I knew everyone was at the pool. Riley's a good girl, yes she is, she wouldn't bark and bark for no reason. I checked on her and let her out to run for a few minutes. Well, she starts sniffing and sniffing. Then she runs into the little space behind that room the boys are always in. And there he was. Your pool toy."

Riley? The Secret Place? Aha! I see.

"Riley?" Coach Greta narrows her eyes. "Who is Riley?"

"Conor's dog," Jack shouts. "I knew you did it!" he happily tells me.

Greta walks toward me. The crowd parts.

"Why did you do it?" Greta stands in front of me, not looking particularly happy.

Coach Monsoon rushes over. "It is important to remember that anger is a force that disturbs the beauty of the world. This wonderful boy is part of the . . ."

"Can it, Mondshine," Greta snaps.

"Bella's brother is a bad guy, Bella's brother is a bad guy," Mugsy singsongs. But not for long.

Bella slugs her.

"I knew it was Conor, didn't I, Timmy?" Jack is so pleased.

"Not now, Jack," I suggest.

"Okay, kid." Greta's face is an inch from mine. "What do you have to say?"

"Two things," I tell her. "I didn't take Sam. And

if I were you I would take a step backward."

"Why?" Greta inches closer.

"Because if you don't back away from my kid right now, I'm gonna feed you this microphone for supper." I could have told her my mom has this thing about her kids.

"I am asking why he took it," Greta and Mom are nose to nose.

"He didn't take it." Go, Mom.

"Why is it in your backyard?"

"I know who took it," I say.

"My brother knows who took it, my brother knows who took it," Bella singsongs at Mugsy.

"Conor knows?" Coach Monsoon asks.

"This better be good," Greta says.

"Watch it," says my mom.

"We thought the person who took Sam did it so we would lose the Give Sam a Hand contest. So someone else, like the Sharks, would win." I explain. "And we thought that the same person ruined the banner, because they were for the Sharks. But this person isn't trying to help the Sharks win. Or make the Octopi lose. This person simply wants the Octopi *not* to win."

"What are you talking about?" Greta asks.

"If we don't win or lose, we just swim. For fun."

"EXACTLY!" Coach Monsoon screams. "You are such a wonderful boy. You understand. All this terrible competition is so, so . . . terrible. It ruins sports. Why not just swim down to the end of the pool? Why try and beat another person?"

"It *is* called a race," my mom explains.

"Why race? Why? The world is such a beautiful place where we can be happy. And swim. And not try to make more money than someone else. Or swim faster. My studies have shown me this is all wrong. So I took your Sam to show you. And I ripped your horrible poster, and took it to my car. Ta da," she says happily, her arms raised high.

Then Coach Monsoon notices all of us. All looking at her.

"Oops," she says.

"Exactly." Jack knows.

"So you took Sam and ran through our back gate to hide him." I reveal what I finally figured out.

"He was too tall to fit in my car. Then I remembered seeing you come out of the gate one morning. So I rushed and hid the silly thing there." Monsoon explains.

"You tried to get him back this afternoon, didn't you?" While I was looking up Octopus in the Big Book of Underworld Creatures.

"I needed to destroy Sam so all this foolishness would be gone from the world," she explains.

"Mondshine, you're fired," Coach Greta informs her.

"But I still have wonderful research to write."

Monsoon's voice sounds like Bella saying "Na na na boo boo."

"But I still have to call your school," Mom says. "And explain a little about theft and vandalism."

Oops.

"Leave the pool," Greta says.

"Wait." Jack runs after her. "I have a few questions to ask. Are you related to Sam Houston? Is your apartment very bare?"

"I owe you an apology, kid." Greta gives me her hand. I take it. "Let me know if I can do you a favor."

"Actually, you can. I'll explain in a minute if you lend me a piece of paper."

"Can I have one too?" Timmy asks.

What for, I wonder?

"And I appreciate your keeping that microphone to yourself," she tells my mom.

"You're welcome."

With the paper in hand, I ask Greta my question. And a few other people in the pool.

I hear Timmy ask my mom, "Have you always been a painter?"

Jack teaches Bubba the towel hula.

Timmy writes his note.

Six people try to take the tape off Dwayne.

And another Freaky Joe case comes to a close.

Chapter Twelve

Nine Plus Ten Plus Five

Two days later, I am ready. The sun shines down on the beautiful world as I stand at the end of the pool.

Putting on my goggles, I face Sam down at the end of the pool.

"Got your list, sport?" Greta asks.

"Ten sponsors," I tell her. I hand her the list.

"Let her rip."

I dive. Swim up. Slap Sam's hand. The crowd chants my name. I know they'll soon run out of breath. And I'll be here all alone. With eighty more laps to do.

Seems like a lot of back and forth. Which I keep doing as

Mom
Mikey
Bella
Dwayne
Timmy
Pablo
Jack
Bubba
Mugsy
Greta

cheer me on.

My sponsors. Each one will give me one dime if I swim one hundred laps. Except Mugsy, who says that is too much. She's giving me a nickel.

But I'm giving Sam a hand.

. . . .

And so that is how it was on our second case. I have written it down here in the book. So one day the story may be known.

I add one more thing to The Secret Files of the Freaky Joe Club.

A note.

The note I was given later, on the day of my swim.

Timmy came to The Secret Place.

"Remember what you said: 'I know I know something, I just don't know what I know,'" he asks.

"Yup."

"Ditto." Timmy hands me the piece of paper he wrote at the pool.

"Here's what I know. But I don't know what I know," he says. "But I can't stay now, 'cause I'm baby-sitting Dwayne." Timmy waves behind him as he leaves.

I read:

Conor's mom called him The Condor.
Conor's mom knew what Conor
meant when he said The Secret Place.

I fold the note, placing it in the files. The Freaky Joe Club will have another meeting. And Timmy and I will talk.

But now, I pick up *Remington Reedmarsh and The Terrible Tyrant*. I wonder how the forces of good will ever win the next battle.

But I'm about to find out. There is nothing like a good mystery.

Want another good mystery?
Coming Soon:

The Freaky Joe Club

Secret File #3:

The Mystery of the Morphing Hockey Stick

THIRD-GRADE DETECTIVES

Everyone in the third grade loves the new teacher, Mr. Merlin.

Mr. Merlin used to be a spy, and he knows all about secret codes and the strange and gross ways the police solve mysteries.

YOU CAN HELP DECODE THE CLUES AND SOLVE THE MYSTERY IN THESE OTHER STORIES ABOUT THE THIRD-GRADE DETECTIVES:

#1 The Clue of the Left-handed Envelope

#2 The Puzzle of the Pretty Pink Handkerchief

#3 The Mystery of the Hairy Tomatoes

#4 The Cobweb Confession

#5 The Riddle of the Stolen Sand

#6 The Secret of the Green Skin

#7 The Case of the Dirty Clue

#8 The Secret of the Wooden Witness

#9 The Case of the Sweaty Bank Robber

  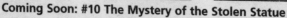

Coming Soon: #10 The Mystery of the Stolen Statue

Harold's not the only canine writer in the
Monroe household—it's the playful dachshund
pup Howie's turn to tell his stories in the

SERIES!

Read them all!